To G. K. Chesterton
with esteem from

Holbrook Jackson.

The Crossways,
Mill Hill N.W.

PLATITUDES IN THE MAKING

By the Same Writer

Platitudes in the Making
Precepts and Advices
for Gentlefolk

By

HOLBROOK JACKSON

LONDON   D. J. RIDER   1911
MITCHELL KENNERLEY   NEW YORK

Ignatius Press
wishes to thank
Dr. Alfred R. and Charlotte Kessler
for the discovery of this book
in the autumn of 1955
in a used bookstore in San Francisco
and for their generosity
in sharing this
literary gem
with the many admirers
of G.K. Chesterton
worldwide

Holbrook Jackson's
Platitudes in the Making
© The Society of Authors, 1911, 1997

With the permission of
A.P. Watt Ltd.
On behalf of
The Royal Literary Fund

Cover design by Roxanne Mei Lum

Reprinted in 1997 by Ignatius Press, San Francisco
All rights reserved
ISBN 0-89870-628-9
Library of Congress catalogue number 96-78010
Printed in the United States of America ∞

These thoughts were written down for my own pleasure. They are now published for the same reason.

All ideas aspire to the condition of platitude.

Contents

Contents

PRELIMINARY PRECEPTS
FOR THOSE ABOUT TO
LIVE

To
THE TWENTY-FIRST CENTURY
AND AFTER

Preliminary Precepts

I.

As soon as an idea is accepted it is time to reject it. *No: it is time to build another idea on it. You are always rejecting: & you build nothing.*

II.

Truth and falsehood in the abstract do not exist.

Then nothing else does

III.

Truth is one's own conception of things. *The Big Blunder. ~~Recedes~~. All thought is an attempt to discover if one's own conception is true or not.*

IV.

A lie is that which you do not believe.

This is a lie : so perhaps you don't believe it

V.

Genius is initiative on fire. *Good*

VI.

Altruism is another name for Egoism.

Both are another name for Nonconformist Conscience

VII.

Originality is only variation.

True. And needs tradition

VIII.

Negations without affirmations are worthless.

And impossible

IX.

Fear of corrupting the mind of the younger generation is the loftiest form of cowardice. *But I prefer it to the arrogance of modern parents who cannot believe that they could ever corrupt anybody.*

X.

In multitude of counsel there is confusion. *Yes: there is frequently. But a mob can drill itself — at least in France*

XI.

Definitions put a limit to ideas; institutions put a limit to life. So long as we recognise these two precepts, both definitions and institutions may be used with advantage. *Definitions are ideas. A snake's head or tail dont "limit" the snake. They make him*

XII.

"No opinion matters finally: except your own." *said the man who thought he was a rabbit.*

XIII.

All things are possible: but not probable. *Good*

XIV.

Familiarity breeds not contempt, but indifference. *But it can breed surprise. Try saying "Boots" ninety times*

XV.

Things done on principle are things done wrong.

Only on the wrong principle; this last principle, for instance.

XVI.

There is nothing old under the sun.

Very good

ADVICES FOR THE SAME

To

C. Haldane Macfall

who does not

need them

Advices

I.

Look after the Real: the Ideal can take care of itself. *And of us?*

II.

Be contented, when you have got all you want. *Till then: be happy*

III.

When dealing with humanity remember you have to make the best of a bad job. *See Fall, Doctrine of*

IV.

Don't think—do.

Do think! Do!

V.

When in doubt, risk it.

But in faith you will risk more.

VI.

Forgive everybody but yourself.

Very good.

VII.

Beware of those who agree with you.

.... True: but dont alter your opinion to annoy them, like Bernard Shaw.

VIII.

Don't try to convert the elderly person :
circumvent him. *And Comprehend.*

IX.

Be sure your kindness is not cowardice.

Right.

X.

Suffer fools gladly : they may be right.

Very good

XI.

Treat the crowd as if you knew best :
its units as if they did. *Be Careful. You might
End in the Cabinet.*

XII.

Go to the ant, thou sluggard, consider
her ways and beware !   *Excellent*

THE INNER TEMPLE

To
FREDERICK NIVEN

The Inner Temple

I.

No two men have exactly the same religion : a church, like society, is a compromise. *The same religion has the two men. The sun shines on the evil & the good. But the sun does not compromise.*

II.

Theology and religion are not the same thing. When the churches are controlled by the theologians religious people stay away. *"Theology is simply that part of religion that requires brains".*

III.

The object of life is life. *Good. Eternal life, I presume.*

IV.

To a healthy being Death is evil.   It is so easy to die. *Easy without being pleasant.*

V.

To be alive : that is the best thing that can happen to any of us. *Quite true.*

VI.

The theologian is the apologist of death. *Why? Because he proclaims life everlasting?*

VII.

The desire for immortality is the human tragedy.   The desire to be loved for one-self the human comedy. *Both are the Divine Comedy.*

VIII.

There is no to-morrow for those who are alive : for the dead, no to-day. *All right, all right.*

IX.

A man is a ship : his religion a harbour.
Few men sail the high seas. *No* ~~men~~ *men do, Except
to find a harbour somewhere.*

X.

All dogmas are right : but it is wrong
to need them. *All men need them, except the
feeble-minded.*

XI.

Doubt is the prerogative of the intellect ;
Faith, of the emotions.   Nowadays the
emotions have all the Doubt and the intellect all the Faith. *The mind exists not to doubt
but to decide.*

XII.

Sacrifice is a form of bargaining. *And bargaining of
sacrifice: but in modern commerce it is human sacrifice*

XIII.

Aspiration is discontent.
*No. Discontent is a negative & even trivial
by-product of aspiration. All modern*

GODS OF THE TWILIGHT

To
JOHN MAVROGORDATO

Gods of the Twilight

I.

The gods are the progeny of the poets :
the poets are the children of all. *Ask the poets*

II.

The god of theology : a power that
creates to destroy. *No : that is obviously the god
of modern science.*

III.

Once you become a Christian you admit
that the kingdom of God is within. The
question then is not whether you believe
in God ; but whether you believe in
yourself. *And you don't. You are not
so babyishly credulous as all that.*

IV.

Desire to please God is never disinterested. *Well, I should hope not.*

V.

God is conservative ; Satan, progressive. Both are useful to the judicious, though necessary only to the feeble. *Is a man feeble because he "needs" Exercise?*

AMORALITIES

To

Eduardo Bolio de Rendon

Amoralities

I.

Goodness and happiness are synonymous terms in a healthy animal. *True: & man is never a healthy animal.*

II.

In the beginning morals were expedients. Later they became institutions. It is only when they are useless that it is necessary to defend them. *In the beginning I wasn't there. But now morals are not useless; nor are they institutions. They are passions.*

III.

Morality is the child of self-consciousness. *No wonder self-consciousness is a little vain. A fine child.*

IV.

Morals are only the rules of communities. They should be judged by their results. *Why "only"?*

V

"Expedients are the only real substitute for morals. *" from" On The Matter in Mayfair: The diary of a Rising Politician" Privately printed.*

VI

Beware of your habits. The better they are the more surely will they be your undoing. *Don't be morbid.*

VII.

Excess is wrong when it negatives itself. ~~░░░░░░░░~~ *It always does.*

VIII.

We are more inclined to regret our virtues than our vices; but only the very honest will admit this.

I dont regret any virtues, except those I have lost.

IX.

Those who preach salvation as a reward for virtue are spiritual hucksters —tradesmen of the soul. *A fallacy. Virtue does not buy salvation:* ~~it~~ *it produces it.*

X.

The first of rights is the right to enjoy. *Granted*

XI.

Those who are careless of happiness are happy. *But be careful in choosing your carelessness.*

XII.

Your readiest desire is your path to joy—even if it destroy you. *No: unless you enjoy being destroyed. Some (rimrunners do).*

XIII.

People who want to be amused have lost the art of living. *Excellent.*

XIV.

Life is great when it is tragic ; but tragedy is born of joy, not sorrow.

Good

XV.

Once you are conscious of real joy, Death, for you, is dead. Those only who have known joy have lived. Joy is the nihilism of consciousness.

This might be turned round. Death is not dead for any of us. The hour comes when Death will be very much alive: the awful hour when Death will be more alive than we. Are we then to deduce that we cannot touch perfect joy till after that has happened?

INHUMANITIES

To

ALL WHO ARE WEARY AND
HEAVY LADEN

Inhumanities

I.

It is easy to be human; but humanism is a dismal failure: look at man. *Look at him; but don't look down at him. Verily I say unto you many prophets & professors have desired to be human beings & have not attained to it.*

II.

Why did Nature create man? Was it to show that she is big enough to make mistakes; or was it pure ignorance?

Nature did not create man. Discuss this.

III.

Man is Nature's first protest against herself; he is a creature suffering from inverted ego. *Otherwise called Swank.*

IV.

Man is a dog's ideal of what God should be. *Sure?*

V.

Man is the only animal that can be a fool. In this there is hope. Folly may be the loophole of retreat. *Very good.*

VI.

There are two kinds of men; those who are the subjects and those who are the lords of their environment. But real power transcends environment. *The good sculptor enjoys marble. It is the vulgar sculptor who tries to transcend it.*

VII.

Mankind reveals itself in civilization. What a revelation! *Quite so. But better than hiding the human spirit, as in some races. The Hindus, for instance, are slaves to the vice of secret thinking.*

VIII.

The future will look upon man as we look upon the ichthyosaurus—as an extinct monster. *The "future" won't look upon anything. No eyes.*

IX.

As soon as a nation becomes civilized it dies ; yet man has but one idea—to become civilized. Thus he assists nature to correct her errors. *No nation dies of mere civilization. It dies of progress.*

X.

Domestic animals are inferior animals. Domesticity is the last refuge of the inferior man. *False. The domestic man is as much braver than the loose one as the domestic dog is braver than the fleeing rabbit.*

XI.

There is no such thing as the average man, except in the mass. The mob is everyman. *But there is the normal man. He is invisible, like all gods.*

XII.

The typical man of any nation is the exception. *I dont mind: if he takes care to prove the truth.*

XIII.

Idiosyncrasy is the individual's contribution to life. Vulgarity is the idiosyncrasy of the crowd. *And a jolly thing too.*

XIV.

He who can lead will lead.   Followers
are not necessary.   *Nor are leaders.*
Nothing that is important is necessary.

XV.

Nowadays an eminent man who obeys
the crowd is called leader.   But there
have been few real leaders even in history.
Most so-called leaders have been tuft-
hunters.   *If they were scalp-hunting*
it is all the same. The point is ; why should they lead
people where people don't want to go ?

XVI.

In democracies, those who lead, fol-
low ; those who follow, lead.   *I don't know.*
There are few democracies now. They are not
allowed.

XVII.

The   individual   saves   humanity ;   but
humanity never forgives him.   Humanity
has no faith in herself, and by that fact
shows she is her own best judge.

Who is " the individual " ?
Do tell me.

XVIII.

Nationality is to nations what indivi-
duality is to persons. *True –*

XIX.

Responsibility proves the man : and
so does irresponsibility. *Good.*

THE OUTER TEMPLE

To

A. St. John Adcock

The Outer Temple

I.

Civilized man has decided that he is a social being; but he has not learnt how to be social. Now it is too late. *Dear, dear.*

II.

A social system that cannot be changed cannot be maintained. *It cannot be either, without a fixed ideal or dogmas.*

III.

A State should be a field for the free play of individuals. *Right.*

IV.

Democracy does not necessarily ignore the few; it recognises the many. *Good.*

D

V.

The wise legislator will always leave a loophole through which humanity may pass into something higher.

But he will put it high up—.

VI.

The supremacy of the lawyer in politics is a menace to freedom. *Quite sound.*

VII.

Every custom was once an eccentricity; every idea was once an absurdity.

No, no, no. Some ideas were always absurdities. This is one of them.

VIII.

How can you tell the inferior politician? He always says "You cannot alter human nature." *He also says "We are not as yet advanced enough"* . . . . . .

IX.

Slavery in the last resort is psychological. The slave can always free himself if his desire for freedom is strong enough. *Very good.*

AT THE FRONT

To
FREDERICK RICHARDSON

At the Front

I

Modern commerce is the confidence trick—glorified. *Much glorified?*

II.

Commercial profit is legalised loot. *Not always. It depends on the lawyers*

III.

Riches are made by accident or stupidity, rarely by intelligence. This does not mean that poverty is a virtue. *Very true*

IV.

Only the rich preach content to the poor. *When they are not preaching Socialism.*

V.

The poor can abolish poverty when they have had enough of it. *And when they are ready to be shot.*

VI.

The rich are not so happy as the poor, because they have not learnt the folly of owning things. *If most people not owning is Paradise, we are indeed in Paradise.*

VII.

Shoddy and adulteration are products of poverty. Luxury is a kind of shoddy. *A kind of shoddy is a luxury.*

VIII.

In a community in which there is involuntary starvation every well-fed person is a thief. *No; only Kleptomaniac.*

IX.

" To give people food is just as wrong as to take it from them. Food should not be in any one's gift: it is the first right of man. "

Exit, followed by the blessing of the unassisted beggar!

X.

The State recognises the right to work for a living by making begging for bread illegal; but it reduces this to an absurdity by making begging for work possible. *What you call the "State" is a fellow in a silk hat who happens to find beggars a nuisance, but never a labour a convenience?*

XI.

The only hope for present society lies in the fear of the poor; there will be no hope for the poor until they realise this. *But only fearless men can be feared.*

XII.

There are only two classes in society: those who get more than they earn, and those who earn more than they get. *Yes —*

XIII.

The poor are the only consistent altruists. They sell all that they have and give to the rich. *Excellent.*

XIV.

The man who is content to work all his time for a wage that just keeps him deserves what he gets. *It might be Heaven.*

XV.

Nobody is competent in all things. Obedience is the prerogative of the incompetent. *Yes. Let us all obey — but Whom?*

XVI.

It is only natural you should obey your superiors; but they are not always above. *But your real Superiors often like you to choose for yourself.*

XVII.

He who spends well, saves. *True*

XVIII.

Success is the reward demanded by the inferior. *True; & got.*

XIX.

Success is fortuitous—and useless. *Success, like progress, means nothing by itself.*

XX.

Charity corrupts both receiver and
giver.   The philanthropist is a symptom
of disease. *What have philanthropist to do
with charity?*

XXI.

Class distinctions are necessary ; but
not those of to-day. *Well, well, As long as we don't
have an Aristocracy of Intellect & Character, I shan't
mind much.*

XXII.

The Middle Class—Mob+Money.
Dont allude to my family like that

XXIII

Motto of the average man : Martyrdom
should never begin at home. *But home is
full of perils.*

XXIV.

The two most admiral qualities of
the working-man are his love of play
and his hatred of intellect.   Such qualities give him a touch of paganism that
makes him kin with the gods. *What he hates
is Intellectualism — the "Intelligenzia"
of Russia. So do I. There is plenty of
intellect in omnibus Conductor's chaff.*

STATEWORTHINESS

To

THE FABIAN SOCIETY

Stateworthiness

I.

Socialism aspires to make the world a
place fit for supreme beings.   Modern
civilization provides no place for them. *There will always
be only one place for supreme beings; outside the city &
called the place of the skull.*

II.

The individual saves the State.   Socialism invites the State to return the com-
pliment.   *But Baal has gone a hunting.*

III.

Socialism recognises that there are
limits to human trustworthiness, and, as
a consequence, seeks to abolish private
property.   This is an admission that no
men are fit to own things. *Exactly. Socialism
is Manichaean & castrates men to keep
them pure. The Catholic Church permitted
Love & Ownership, although they were certain
to produce dangers & sins. Socialism refuses
this courageous course & goes back to the ——
desert with the pessimists*

IV.

Laisser faire made too great a demand on human nature : for that reason it failed. Socialism will succeed because it does not expect too much of men. *It expects too little. It will have a surprise.*

V.

Socialism is the only thing that will save us from collectivism—except, of course, commercialism. *Socialism means the amalgamation of Whitely's with Harrod's Stores. I don't like either.*

THE RED CAP

To
M. D. Eder

The Red Cap

I.

Revolution is the flower of evolution.

The Tree seems withered

II.

Revolutions begin in the spirit : with man they generally end there.   *with modern enlightened man , yes.*

III.

Force is sometimes on the side of revolt ; but it is always on the side of institutions.   *Force without Courage is useless on either side.*

E

IV.

Insurrections are revolutions at exploding point ; they are caused by incompetent statesmanship. *Or too Competent.*

V.

Insurrection may force the pace of reform, but personal example makes reform more certain. *Death is the best personal example —*

VI.

We are all revolutionists when we are young— —when we are young we are wise. *Good.*

VII.

The great revolution of the future will be Nature's revolt against man. *I hope Man will not hesitate to shoot.*

FOR THOSE IN LOVE

To

LA FEMME AUX YEUX VERTS

OF MATISSE

For Those in Love

I.

Love is the most subtle form of self-interest. *Sly dog.*

II.

Love flatters, so does Art.   Love and Art are the creative faculties. *Insinuating Buck!*

III.

Modern love enslaves; but that is not an objection if you like it. ~~tolerate~~ *Thanks; I like it in reason.*

IV.

Love has become a soporific.   People take to it as they take to drink. *They don't get it, then.*

V.

When we love we are most like
animals. When we love we are at our
best. *We are never like animals.
And least of all in love.*

VI.

Women cannot be impersonal; that
is why they are irresistable—and detest-
able. *Yes.*

VII.

Woman is not undeveloped man; but
man is. *Witty. Two marks.*

VIII.

Marriage among the middle classes is
a bargain. Among the free it would be
a compromise. *Sofa*

IX.

The marriage system created a new
sport—adultery. *Yes; a cruel sport.*

X.

Love is protective only when it is free.

Love is never free.

XI.

The procreative side of life is Nature's device, not man's. Man has to be seduced into reproducing his kind by pleasure. But in the sterilisation of marriage he takes his revenge. *On himself.*

XII.

Modesty in Nature is protective ; in civilization it is seductive. *It is always beautiful.*

XIII.

The most hopeful sign of the present age is the decline of the birth rate.

Christ! What an age!

SLIPPING THE CABLES

To
WILFRED WHITTEN
(malgré lui)

Slipping the Cables

I.

"Reason is the dotage of instinct." *said the sheep haughtily as they followed each other to the slaughter-house*

II.

Ideas are not the product of thought;✱
they are flashes of light from the un-
known. Deliberation is barren.

✱ *Some ideas aren't.*

III.

Thought and imagination together are
the masters of destiny : apart they must
ever remain its slaves. *True . Go up three places*

IV.

Man cannot rest till he knows every-
thing ; but not through the intellect.

Why this intolerance of the human intellect ?

V.

Intelligence is ability to vary your habits. *Yes; by perceiving some ideal standard above habit. Intelligence is the form of dogmatising rightly.*

VI.

He who reasons is lost. *He who never reasons is not worth finding.*

VII.

Only stupid people are wholly sane. *No people are wholly sane. But the wise are saner than the stupid.*

VIII.

All merely brainy people are duffers. *Yes; like all merely leggy people.*

IX.

Cleverness and genius are not the same thing. *But they are both trifles.*

LAYING THE DUST

To
LOVAT FRASER

Laying the Dust

I.

The academic person is an intellectual sycophant. *Why not say "intellectual"?*

II.

The academic attitude is always obsolete. *I wish the word "obsolete" were obsolete.*

III.

" Academies sometimes honor genius, but cannot cultivate or protect it." *from "Dialogues of the Dons: or Balliol & Merton Unmasked" Privately printed.*

VI.

The sum total of critical opinion is *nil*. Critics cancel each other. *Only when the critics are vulgar factions.*

V.

Pedants are the peddlers of intellect. *Will no peddler protest against this? Do you think a pedant only peddle? It is a romantic & dangerous trade.*

BETWEEN OURSELVES

To
DAN RIDER

Between Ourselves

I.

A man's spiritual kin are his nearest relations. *See parallel passage in the Gospel, more paradoxically put.*

II.

Friendship is mutual curiosity. *Quite right, as long as it isn't gratified.*

III.

Friendship is the only respectable form of human intimacy.

Puritan!

HERE'S JOY !

A Vous

Here's Joy !

I.

It is lésé Dionysos to drink wine for
the purpose of quenching thirst. *It depends on
the wine. Claret is meant to quench, Port to
warm, Champagne only exhilarates; it is therefore
a little unmanly.*

II.

To drink to forget is to abuse drink.

*Thoroughly sound. One
should drink to remember.*

PRELUDE TO ART

To
JOSEPH SIMPSON

Prelude to Art

I.

Art expresses the phases of life we are unable to live. It is the sign of a limited consciousness. *Good — But all consciousness is limited.*

II.

Great art anticipates life. *Good*

III.

In degenerate ages the arts are pastimes. *In perfectly putrid ages they are taken seriously.*

IV.

In a beautiful city an art gallery would be superfluous. In an ugly one it is a narcotic. *In a real one it is an art gallery.*

V.

A renaissance is an epidemic of theft.

VI.

In a society worthy the name all men would be artists—without knowing it.

They all are: but without your knowing it.

VII.

One should not despise enthusiasm for the commonplace in art if one loves the people—because, in it the people see themselves reflected.

Enough is too much : but too little is not enough.

BOOKS BY

HOLBROOK JACKSON

GREAT ENGLISH NOVELISTS

BY HOLBROOK JACKSON

"Mr. Holbrook Jackson's addition to this useful series of the lives of eminent Englishmen is quite an admirable one, and will tell many people as much as they need know about the history of the authors in whom they delight. . . . We heartily recommend this book, which is adorned by many illustrations of peculiar interest."—*Daily Telegraph.*

"Mr. Holbrook Jackson has written a plain and pleasant handbook on the great English Novelists. . . . . He seems to us singularly successful in holding the balance between the realists like Defoe, and the idealists like Richardson into which novelists may be roughly divided. He also brings out well the great preponderance of the novels with a purpose in English literature." *Pall Mall Gazette.*

"I think there is more good criticism crammed into this book than any that was spread loose through his book on Bernard Shaw, where he could splash about in the featureless future. . . . . Just as Mr. Jackson would have liked to write a book on every one of his novelists, so I should like to write an article upon almost every one of Mr. Jackson's paragraphs."

G. K. CHESTERTON in *The Daily News.*

GRANT RICHARDS 3s. 6d. net.

BERNARD SHAW

A Monograph

BY HOLBROOK JACKSON

"Mr. Holbrook Jackson has written a really interesting and capable book on 'G.B.S.,' which is all the better for being also quite enthusiastic and quite one-sided. Many will probably sneer at him for treating his subject so completely in the spirit of a partisan: they will certainly be wrong. Mr. Bernard Shaw is not only a brave, a detatched, and yet a responsible man, but he has this great quality about him, that men are for him or against him. You cannot write an impartial life of Shaw any more than of Mahomet. I do not blame Mr. Holbrook Jackson for arguing for 'G.B.S.' He must have argued either for him or against him. He would have written better philosophy if he had argued against him, but he has written good literature even in arguing for him .... the very fact that Mr. Holbrook Jackson's work moves the mind to destructive reflections is only a further proof of the splendid sincerity and intellectual sympathy which really shines through his pages. It is the study of a great man made in the great spirit of loyalty and mental watchfulness in which such a study should be made."

G. K. CHESTERTON, in *The Morning Post*.

GRANT RICHARDS 5s. net. Cheap edition 1s. net.

EVERYCHILD

A Book of Verse for Children

EDITED BY

HOLBROOK JACKSON

This Volume is designed to appeal to the imagination of children.

It contains poems by W. B. YEATS, RUD-YARD KIPLING, W. H. DAVIES, GERALD GOULD, HENRY NEWBOLT, WILLIAM MORRIS, ROBERT LOUIS STEPHENSON, CHARLES DAL-MON, EUGENE FIELD, and others.

J. W. BEAN, LEEDS   6d. net.

Printed Privately by
A. T. Stevens
London